ook
>26

Cat and the Beanstalk

written by Charlotte Guillain ☆ illustrated by Dawn Beacon

Chicago, Illinois

© 2014 Raintree
an imprint of Capstone Global Library, LLC
Chicago, Illinois

To contact Capstone Global Library please call 800-747-4992, or visit our web site
www.capstonepub.com

Edited by Daniel Nunn, Rebecca Rissman, and Catherine Veitch
Designed by Joanna Hinton-Malivoire
Original illustrations © Capstone Global Library, Ltd, 2014
Illustrated by Dawn Beacon
Production by Victoria Fitzgerald
Originated by Capstone Global Library, Ltd
Printed and bound in China

17 16 15
10 9 8 7 6 5 4 3 2

Library of Congress Cataloging-in-Publication Data
Guillain, Charlotte.
  Cat and the beanstalk / Charlotte Guillain.
     pages cm—(Animal fairy tales)
  ISBN 978-1-4109-6113-6 (hb)—ISBN 978-1-4109-6120-4 (pb) [1. Fairy tales. 2. Folklore—
England. 3. Giants—Folklore.] I. Jack and the beanstalk. English. II. Title.
  PZ8.G947Cat 2014
  398.2—dc23   2013011475
  [E]

Characters

Cat

Giant Dog

Cat's Mother

Old Weasel

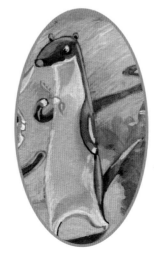

There was once a young kitten named
Cat who lived with his mother. They
were very poor.

One day, things had gotten so bad that
Cat's mother sent him to the market
to sell their cat basket.

On the way to the market, Cat met an old weasel.

"Where are you going?" asked the weasel.

"I'm going to the market to sell our cat basket," replied Cat.

"I'll give you three magic beans for your cat basket," said the weasel. Cat agreed and hurried home to show the beans to his mother.

But Cat's mother was very angry
when she saw the magic beans. She
threw them out of the window. Cat
and his mother went to sleep feeling
hungry and uncomfortable without
any food or their basket.

Cat's mother was very happy when she saw the golden cans.
"Go back up tomorrow and see what else you can find," she told him.

So the next morning, Cat climbed up the beanstalk again. He sneaked back into the giant dog's room in the castle.

This time, Cat found a pile of glittering golden pet collars! Cat could hear the giant dog snoring again, but he picked up the collars and tiptoed away without waking him.

Cat climbed back down the beanstalk, and his mother was delighted with the golden collars.

The next morning, Cat's mother was
pointing at the beanstalk again.
"Go back up and see what else you can
find!" she said.

So Cat climbed back up the beanstalk and
sneaked back into the castle. In the giant
dog's room was a pile of magic pet toys.
As the dog snored, Cat filled his bag and
started to tiptoe away.

Cat crept to the top of the beanstalk and was about to climb down when the golden toys in his bag started to rattle! Cat froze as he heard the sound of the giant dog barking from the castle.

"Fee-fi-fo-fat,
I smell the blood of a furry cat!
Be he orange or striped or black,
I'll eat him for my morning snack!"

Cat heard the giant dog running after him. He hurried down the beanstalk, with the toys rattling loudly in his bag. When Cat got to the bottom, he grabbed an ax and chopped the beanstalk down. He was safe!

CHOP!

Cat and his mother were rich. They lived happily ever after, and Cat never had to go on an adventure ever again.

The End

Where does this story come from?

You've probably already heard the story that *Cat and the Beanstalk* is based on—*Jack and the Beanstalk*. There are many different versions of this story. When people tell a story, they often make little changes to make it their own. How would you change this story?

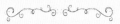

The history of the story

Jack and the Beanstalk is an English folktale that was told by oral storytellers for many years before it was written down. Storytellers entertained people in the days before radio and television. The story was written down in various collections, such as Joseph Jacobs's *English Fairy Tales* in 1890.

The original story tells of a young boy, Jack, who lives with his mother, who is a widow. They are very poor. When their cow stops providing them with milk, Jack's mother sends him to the market to sell the animal. On the way to the market, an old man gives Jack some magic beans for the cow, but Jack's mother is furious when he returns home without any money. She throws the beans out of the window and sends Jack to bed. Overnight a giant beanstalk grows, and in the morning Jack climbs it. At the top is a strange land where a giant lives. The giant's wife gives Jack some food, but when the giant smells him, Jack has to hide to avoid being eaten. He steals a bag of gold and escapes down the beanstalk. Jack returns two more times and is helped by the giant's wife before he steals a hen that lays golden eggs, and then a magic harp. When he steals the harp, it plays music and alerts the giant, who almost catches Jack. Then Jack escapes by chopping down the beanstalk and killing the giant. Jack and his mother live happily ever after and are never poor again.